W9-BSQ-018

Published by Scholastic Inc.
90 Old Sherman Turnpike, Danbury, Connecticut 06816.

For information regarding permission, write to:
Disney Licensed Publishing
114 Fifth Avenue, New York, New York 10011.

ISBN 0-7172-6820-9

Designed and produced by Bill SMITH STUDIO.

Printed in the U.S.A.
First printing, May 2004

Teatime Trouble

A Story About
Respect

by **Jacqueline A. Ball**
illustrated by
Duendes del Sur

SCHOLASTIC INC.

New York   Toronto   London   Auckland   Sydney
Mexico City   New Delhi   Hong Kong   Buenos Aires

"This room is so peaceful," Aladdin said, looking around the sunny room.

"Father loves this room, too," Jasmine added. "He had it specially decorated to match the lilies in the garden. That is why he calls it the Hall of Lilies."

"*I* could stay here all day," said Aladdin. "You could if you did not have to go with Father," Jasmine reminded him. Aladdin and Jasmine's father, the Sultan, were taking a short trip into the desert to buy some camels.

"*W*e will have dinner here tonight when you return," Jasmine promised.

Aladdin smiled at his princess. "Good idea."

*J*ust then a gong sounded. Aladdin swallowed some tea and stood up. "Time to go," he said. "Where's Abu?"

"He was right here a minute ago," said Jasmine.

"Oh no!" cried Jasmine. "Father's brand-new silk curtains!"

"Abu!" called Aladdin.

"Get off! Now!"

Holding his tea, Aladdin reached up for Abu. But he tripped over the table and fell, pulling the curtains down. He and Abu landed on the floor, tangled in the tea-soaked, cake-splattered curtains.

"Now look at what you've done, Abu!" exclaimed Aladdin. He looked helplessly at the mess. "I mean, look at what *we've* done."

"*I*t was just an accident," Jasmine consoled.
She began to pick up the mess.

"Here, let me help you," said Aladdin.

"No, the gong has sounded. You need to hurry,
and you must change your clothes. Do not
worry—I will fix everything."

After Aladdin left, Jasmine cleaned up the room and examined the curtains. The delicate silk was stained and torn.

"There is no way these can be repaired," she finally decided. "We will have to make new ones. Maybe the royal seamstress can help."

*B*ut then she had a thought. "Aladdin will be embarrassed if anyone learns what happened. I will have to solve this problem alone."

She scooped up Abu. "Come on. We need to find some more of this lily-patterned silk."

At the bazaar, Jasmine stopped at
the first stall and began to sort through
many different kinds of cloth.

*I*n no time, Abu was bored. He grabbed a banana and sat down on some carpets to peel it.

"*T*hat monkey took my banana!" a customer yelled, glaring at Abu.

"*A*nd he's sitting on *my* carpets," a merchant added angrily.

"*O*h, Princess Jasmine!" the customer and merchant exclaimed together, when they recognized her.

"Abu meant no harm," Jasmine said quietly. "But he should not have taken or used anyone else's property."

"*A*bu, we have to respect other people's belongings and property. So you cannot take things that belong to someone else," Jasmine explained to Abu. "Nor can you make yourself at home in a merchant's stall."

Abu nodded, trying to understand.

*J*asmine kept walking from stall to stall. She
found silk with cactus flowers . . .

. . . silk with tiger stripes . . .

. . . silks as green as jade . . .

. . . and as blue as the sea . . .
But she found no silk with
the Sultan's lily pattern.

She sighed. "Maybe we won't be able to replace the curtains after all," Jasmine thought. "Poor Aladdin will feel terrible. And Father will be disappointed, too."

Suddenly she felt a tug on her skirt. Abu was frantically chattering, jumping up and down, and pointing across the bazaar.

*I*n a far-off stall, Jasmine could see bolts of beautiful material. She peered more closely. A bolt standing in front of the stall had the Sultan's lily pattern!

"Oh, thank you, Abu!" she exclaimed. She grabbed his hand and rushed towards the stall.

$\mathcal{B}$ut along the way, she heard someone call her name.

"Princess Jasmine!" She turned and saw Hakim, an elderly man who had once driven camels for the Sultan. Hakim was famous for telling long stories about his adventures in the desert many years ago.

Abu pulled on Jasmine's hand impatiently. "I know we are in a hurry, Abu," Jasmine whispered. "But we must be polite and respectful." So although she had little time, Jasmine kindly asked, "How are you, Hakim?"

"*I* could be better, Princess Jasmine," Hakim replied. "My back acts up in weather like this. It's an old injury I got escaping a gang of thieves in the desert. . . . "

Jasmine listened patiently, trying to ignore Abu's frantic motions, as Hakim talked on and on.

When Hakim finally finished, Abu dragged Jasmine away, chattering loudly.

"I want the silk, too, Abu," Jasmine said. "But few things are as important as showing our elders respect. We have much to learn from them."

But by the time they reached the stall, another customer was admiring the lily silk!

Abu covered his eyes. Jasmine fought back a cry of disappointment.

"Princess!" the merchant called. "I almost didn't see you. Come to the front of the line."

*I*f Jasmine went ahead of the other customer, the silk was hers. If she waited her turn, it could be gone. And she had no time to look for more.

What would a princess do?

Jasmine shook her head no. Going to the front of the line would not show respect for the other customer.

"I'll wait my turn," she said.

*J*asmine waited nervously as the customer picked up the lily silk, put it back down, examined other material, picked up the lily silk again . . . until finally, she chose another pattern!

Beaming with happiness, Jasmine bought the lily silk. Then she and Abu raced back to the palace. "We'll have to work fast, Abu," she told him. Abu chattered that he would help.

*J*asmine, Abu, and even the Magic Carpet
worked very hard for the rest of the afternoon.

$\mathcal{F}$inally, the new curtains were hung. Jasmine
looked at them carefully. "They look okay to me,"
she said.

Just then Aladdin walked in. "They look great,"
he said, hugging Jasmine. "Thank you!"

That night after dinner, the Sultan leaned back and looked around the Hall of Lilies. "This room looks wonderful," he said. "Don't you think so, Aladdin?"

"Better than ever," Aladdin said, smiling at Princess Jasmine.

The End